The Uninvited Guests

The Uninvited Guests

by

David Keyes

A Cecil Herbert Woolley Mystery

THE HOUSE OF POMEGRANATES PRESS

Published by The House of Pomegranates Press
www.houseofpomegranates.ca

ISBN 978-0-9784543-7-1

Set in Adobe Garamond Pro and
ITC Luna

Garamond is an old style serif typeface originally cut by
Glaude Garamond for the Parisian scholar-printer Robert Estienne in the first part of
the sixteenth century. The Garamond font used in the text of this book was designed by
Robert Slimbach for Adobe Systems in 1989.
ITC Luna is the work of Japanese designer Akira Kobayashi who was inspired by the
designs of the 1930s.

Designed in 2017 by Gillian Holmes of
The House of Pomegranates Press
and typeset in Toronto on an iMac computer.
Copyedited by Jean Nielsen.

For Mr. Squirrel

The
Uninvited
Guests

Chapter One

The sinewy craft glided further out to sea, the smell of burnt suntan oil, French cigarettes and cheap alcohol dissipating with each nautical yard. In the fading twilight, the moon was huge and the water an inky blue, behind them the lights of St. Tropez slowly blurred into a haze. The air was a perfect olfactory mix of ocean brine and jasmine blown by coastal breezes. Ahead was their destination, which looked less an island and more like the shadowy head and shoulders of an enormous giant. Lounging in the second seat Cecil Herbert Woolley, clothed in a white linen suit and silk bow tie, crossed his legs and decorously smoked a cigarette. Beside him Clemency de la Tour, elegantly dressed in an shimmering silver shift that dipped far too low in the front and even lower in the back, sat with her eyes closed, breathing in the night, her golden hair flowing behind her.

"Rum this Clem," shouted Cecil over the motor and the spray, "What sort of night have you got us into? I didn't know there was an island off the coast let alone an inhabited one."

Clemency dreamily opened her eyes, "Cecil, I told

you about this weeks ago."

"You did?"

"Yes."

"Must have forgot. Can you give me the gist?"

"You remember Cecilia, my cousin from the west?"

"Vaguely."

"Well, she is 21 today and we are fêting her."

"Meaning?"

"A party."

"Meaning?"

"Relatives."

"Oh Good Lord Clemency, you didn't tell me there were relatives involved! I thought this trip to the South of France was just a jaunt but now I find it's a calculated coup d'etat."

"I'm sorry Darling, I didn't mean to spring them on you like this. I had hoped to remain a mystery forever but this is unavoidable… and I promised. And you must meet Aunt Hattie. You must!"

"Aunt Hattie? Oh Lord! I am not prepared. I, too, had hoped to remain a mystery, at least to your relatives. Honestly darling… no! No! We are not going to this party." Cecil stood and tapped the shoulder of the pilot. "My good man, I demand you turn this craft around immediately and head for home!"

The man smiled at him.

"I say, on the double, turn this craft around before we are spotted!"

"Darling," Clemency said, pulling Cecil back down onto the seat, "he's Serbian. Unless you can speak Serbian, we've got no choice." Clemency turned to the pilot and spoke to him in Serbian. The man chuckled and reaching into his jacket, pulled out a flask and with a wink handed it to Woolley.

Woolley took the flask and drank. The liquid burned, "My God!"

The pilot laughed and said something to Clemency who also laughed.

"Going to translate that?" asked Woolley handing back the flask.

"Probably better not to."

Suddenly the island's dock came into view, lit by a string of electrical bulbs that had been hung along it for a festive feel. The Serb deftly maneuvered the boat up to the quayside beside a small ornate boathouse, where valets in crisp, nautical looking uniforms grabbed the ropes and pulled the craft to a standstill.

"Well darling," Clemency said as she took the hand of one of the dock valets, "we are here."

"It's not too late to turn back. I have a lot of cash. I will bribe our boatsman and we will make a getaway."

"Please darling, do this for me. I'm sure there will be a spectacularly stocked bar." She turned and started walking ahead. "Think of this as a free night out."

"It's my soul darling," called Cecil as he stepped up onto the dock and straightened his suit. "I worry for my soul."

"*Смрт путује брзо*," said the driver as he started up the boat, quickly spinning it around and back out to sea.

"Good Lord," thought Cecil as he watched the boat head out into the night. "How dramatic!" Turning back he was surprised to see that Clemency was gone.

"Darling," he shouted, "Do wait." Hurrying down the dock he yelled again, "Darling, don't leave me here. Do wait up."

Chapter Two

The dock ended at an ancient stone wall. Cecil could just make out an iron trellis and gate, rusted by the salt air and overgrown with vines. He stumbled through the postern, the gate creaking ominously with his push, and he found himself at the beginning of a gravel path that wound steeply into a dark, lush forest. The air grew stagnant, the dense vegetation exhaling a sickly smell of rot. The forest floor was covered in brown pine needles; fireflies twinkled and glowed. The path was lit by strings of lights that created a preternatural glow too dim to be of actual use, while stones that had been set along the path for ease of walking were separated just enough to make walking actually quite difficult. Up ahead, Cecil could just make out the shimmering silver of Clemency's dress as she made her way up the steep walk. He quickly caught up with her and they paused on a level patch, huffing and glistening.

"Not what I had in mind…" puffed Cecil, "Definitely not what I call fun."

"Shhh, we're nearly there. Listen! I can hear the ice in the shaker now." Clemency said, by way of encouragement and continued climbing.

Chuffed, Cecil followed, attacking the steps with

renewed vim. "Darling," he called out.

"Yes, Cecil."

"You really do have a delicious bottom."

"Thank you, Cecil."

Within minutes the forest gradually thinned to a clearing and there, across glowing expanse of lawn, sat a rather large and very peculiar house.

Clemency and Cecil paused to gain a little composure. Cecil pulled out his handkerchief (as always, crisp and edged in black) and handed it to Clemency.

"Thank you darling." She wiped her brow then took out her compact and reapplied powder. "Do I look a fright?"

"Not at all, darling, not at all," Cecil smiled. "Hmm, it really will be a conundrum."

"What will darling?"

"Why, where to look! What with your lovely bosom so … front and centre you might say, and your lovely face, and your all around lovely behi..."

"Darling, please! Focus!"

"I am focused, I am!"

"I mean on the party, not on my bottom."

Cecil took the handkerchief and wiped his own brow. "If one must…"

"Yes, Cecil, you must. You'll need all your wit and charm for Aunt Hattie. Thankfully the party is not for her, it is for Cecilia and she will have lots of nice young friends getting drunk and vomiting in the shrubbery."

"Ah, to be young again." Cecil pocketed the handkerchief.

"Ready?" asked Clemency

"As I'll ever be."

"Think of the martinis."

"Well," Cecil said, sucking in his breath, "*Nos morituri te salutamus*," and taking Clemency's arm, proceeded out onto the green, which was oddly spongy.

They passed a group of white-coated staff moving about purposefully, setting up small tables here, hanging paper lanterns there. Standing on a makeshift stage and tuning their horns was a swing band.

Cecil whispered to Clemency, "Darling, really. I had no idea you had relatives here, or a family seat, or whatever this pile is fondly referred to."

"It's Aunt Hattie's. She is a staunch communist but, like all of us, comes from money. This was the winter escape for her side of the family. She tried to sell it once to fund an orphanage in India, and another time to produce a Broadway musical about the Diggers. Each time the family lawyers blocked her. And because of that, although she maintains full run of the place, she can make no decisions concerning its wellbeing; she can't even move the furniture. I believe she even had to vet the guest list with the lawyers as one time she held a meeting of anarchists and they got into the wine cellar."

"Well, yes, can you blame them, anarchists and free spirits?"

"The house has been in the family for generations, back to a time when we were pirates."

"Pirates?!"

Clemency laughed, "I come from some of the most blood thirsty stock not sent to Australia. This island was an ideal hiding spot for everything, vessels included. The ocean floor in these parts juts up quite alarmingly in a number of places and if you don't know your way you'll be in for it. On the other side, the side facing the open sea, the cliffs are riddled with caves. One of the caves is large enough to moor a ship and is connected to the house by a secret passageway."

"Goodness."

"Goodness had nothing to do with it," she laughed.

As they made their way to the front path, the band started playing St. James Infirmary. Cecil paused, lit a cigarette, and thought they were quite good.

The house itself was as ancient as it was imposing, with three grand stories of windows and an enormous carved stone entrance. The walls were aged and eaten by the salt air and looked as if they were being held together by barnacles and iron pikes. There were seven lightning rods and four enormous chimneys standing symmetrical and erect along the roof. An observation tower rose up in the middle overlooking the sea, it's widow's walk surrounded by an ornate filigree fence, once black but now rusted. The garden was filled with red flowers that gave the impression of blood bubbling up from below. A girlish voice suddenly shouted. "Clemency! Up here... wait, I'll come down!" It was Cecilia.

Chapter Three

"Clemency!" Cecilia shouted, running down the front steps of the house and onto the gravel. She squealed and threw her arms passionately around Clemency. "You're here! Oh I am ever so grateful that you could come."

"Goodness, Cecilia," said Clemency, startled. "Honestly. I have not come back from the dead, just the Carlton."

Cecilia pulled away and gave Clemency a loving look. "Lord, can you show more cleavage with that dress!"

"Not you too, I'm becoming quite self-conscious."

"No, really, you look quite lovely, I wish I had bosoms like those."

"Really, Cecilia!" chittered Clemency quite pleased.

Cecil, while being ignored, thought Cecilia looked young for her age, boyish and slim, ideal for the times. She wore a white cotton polo top and blue Capri pants, her hair cut into a fashionable bob. She resembled Clemency in many ways – the same cat-like mouth and delicate nose. Her eyes were a startling green.

Cecil cleared his throat.

"Oh, this is Cecil," said Clemency.

"Cecil!" Cecilia shouted, picking him up and twirling

him around.

"Good Lord!" stuttered Cecil. "You're quite the friendly sort."

"I'm just so glad you could come! It's so nice to finally meet the great Cecil Herbert Woolley that I've heard so much about." She punched him and continued, "We all thought Clemency made you up as no one had actually seen you." She pinched him and laughed, "Are you quite real?"

Cecil quickly stepped behind Clemency, "Look here young thing, I'm not very physical. Bruise easily and all that."

"Yes, Cecilia, Cecil is quite a peach," laughed Clemency. "Oh! I'm so glad to see you. The house looks gorgeous! I love the lawn and the decorations. But where are all your chums? Isn't there a party going on?"

"Oh, the gang is in their rooms changing, that's where I was. I spied you from my bedroom. You've just missed cocktails."

Cecil coughed spasmodically.

"But I'm sure there's plenty left for stragglers. You must say hello to Hattie. She's already changed and is in the study talking her Bolshy talk with some professor who's here freeloading. Says he's writing a book. Oh! I must go change. My dress is quite dour, nothing like what you're wearing. I wish I had cleavage like yours Clemency!"

"Again! Honestly, one more remark like that and I'm putting on a sack!"

"Oh come now, cousin! I'm just envious. Go meet momma and then come up and talk to me while I change. Cecil, you can ... occupy yourself? I know I'm being selfish but it's my birthday so I'm allowed."

Cecil cleared his throat, "Oh, I'm sure I can find something to keep me busy."

"Excellent, hurry up then. I'm in my usual room, at the top of the stairs two doors down!"

Cecilia raced off back into the house.

Cecil raised an eyebrow. "Energetic child."

"Well, Aunt Hattie is her mother."

"Are all the de la Tours this ... outgoing?"

"Oh yes, you can count yourself lucky that I am the introverted one." Clemency kissed Cecil on the nose, "Shall we face the music?"

Cecil put out his hands in supplication, "Yes, I am ready."

They locked arms and made their way into the house where they were instantly enveloped in the dark amber light of the entrance hall, a great chilly space with a vaulted wooden ceiling and a floor of patterned black and white marble. Directly in front was the grand staircase, which led to a very large landing strewn with odd bits of furniture, then split and ran up either side of an impressive stained glass window that backed onto a two-storey conservatory. To the left of them was a hall leading to the dining and day rooms, to the right was the door to the library, which took up a full bottom quarter, front to back, of the house. The furniture was all black wood, as was the wainscoting, as were the doors; in fact for a winter escape everything was unusually heavy and oppressive. On the library side there was a huge stone fireplace that Woolley took an instant liking to. "Very Baronial I'd say. Now, which direction do you think the cocktails are in?"

"I'm sure they are with Aunt Hattie."

"Hattie the Bolshy."

"Cecil, shush!"

"Aunt Bolshy."

Clemency took Cecil's hand and they proceeded towards the library, clicking across the marble in their fine shoes. At the door they heard shouting. It was a woman's voice, "You shameless capitalist defector!"

Cecil looked at Clemency, "Unrest!"

"That would be Aunt Hattie," Clemency whispered.

"Sounds in fine form," responded Cecil.

"I want you done and out of my house by midnight. No party for you EX-comrade!" There was a loud thud, and then quite suddenly the library door flew open and a rather attractive man with chiseled features and a large moustache stormed past. He was dressed in a peasant shirt and rough cloth trousers tied with a tie. He trailed a faint hint of patchouli. "I would not even be on a black list with you Hattie de la Tour!" he shouted. "You are not a communist, you are a one person fascist regime!"

A large women with a very round, very red face came to the doorway. She was dressed unflatteringly in greys and mosses; her thin, greying hair was held in a severe bun. "And you are a weasel!" she shouted. "No, I insult weasels! You are a WORM!" Then, noticing Clemency, she squealed, "Oh Good Lord, Clemency!" Breaking into a thunderous laugh, she picked Clemency up off the ground.

"Oh dear, I am detecting a pattern here," mused Cecil.

"And is this…is this…Mr. Cecil Herbert Woolley! As I live and breathe!"

14   **David Keyes**

In an attempt to take charge Cecil put out his hand but Hattie grabbed him bodily and twirled. "I'm so glad you could come. And Clemency, it's been years. Years! You look splendid, look at your cleavage!"

"Aunt Hattie please!"

"Sorry! And Cecil, we all thought…"

"Yes," started Cecil, straightening his clothes once again, "that Clemency made me up. But no, I am here in the flesh so to speak."

"Welcome, welcome. You've missed the cocktails but there is a tray in there, help yourself."

"Ah!" exclaimed Cecil, "Music to my ears," and proceeded into the room.

"Who was that, Aunt Hattie?" asked Clemency.

"Oh, Professor Janek from the University. He is here… ha… WAS here," Hattie leaned past Clemency and bellowed at the top of her lungs, "WAS here! He was here researching a book about communism, capitalism and piracy, the three very elements that make up our family tree. But after a month all he's done is eat, flirt with Cecilia and now, I find, dig into the family's personal finance records in a not very scholarly way."

"Oh dear, do you think he planned to embezzle?"

"He was planning on something, that's why I'm showing him the door." Hattie leaned past Clemency and shouted, "SHOWING HIM THE DOOR!"

In the library Cecil found the drinks tray. He gazed in adoration at the implements: a polished silver shaker that sat glistening in the light; a silver ice bucket filled with irregularly shaped cubes; a crystal measuring glass; an ornate silver bowl filled with olives in brine, and beside it a set of silver swords to spear them. There were three kinds of gin, two vermouths, a silver seltzer bottle and the most delicate martini glasses Cecil had ever seen. The room went silent around him; he thought he might weep when suddenly he was wakened from his reverie by a hard slap on the back.

"So, Cecil," said Hattie, "You've come to make a proper woman of our Clemency. Good man, good man. I hope yours is an egalitarian partnership, work done by equal hands; although a woman, she is equal in every way!"

"Madam, Clemency is more man than I am… more woman also. May I…" he gestured to the drinks tray.

"By all means… by all means. The kids were here. Kids! My baby is 21… kids! Anyhow, they were all drinking drinks with fizz in them. Can't abide by that. Fizz."

"It can come in handy."

"What can?"

"Fizz."

"Ha!" roared Hattie. "Fizz!"

This was going to be a long night thought Cecil.

Chapter Four

Clemency sat on a chair next to the tub smoking a cigarette while Cecilia bathed. Steam rippled down onto the cool tiled floor like fog. The bathroom was huge (having originally been a bedroom) with an enormous tub sitting in the very centre. All the fixtures were ornate brass; everything seemed to have claws. A large semicircular window overlooked the cliff at the back of the house and the open ocean beyond. The floor, like all the floors in the house, was of black wood.

"Oh Clemency, I'm so happy you could come. I know it's all bosh, these milestones, but there really is something about the twenty-first. I'm just so glad we could be together as you're the closest thing to a sister I've got. And to finally meet the famous Cecil… what a handsome devil he is!"

Clemency handed the cigarette to Cecilia. "He is, isn't he? Don't tell Hattie, or anyone for that matter, but I think we might cohabit one day."

Cecilia exhaled, "Lord, that's something I thought I'd never hear from my free-spirited cousin Clem."

"Yes, I can't believe it myself." Clemency attempted an American accent. "Love sure is funny…" then gave up.

"And what about you? Anyone you fancy?"

"Pass the cloth, thanks. No… you know… I mean boys my age seem quite retarded really. I can't relate. And think how we've been raised, you and your father, me and good old Comrade Hattie. We're not like other people. And … frankly …" she hesitated, "I'm just not that interested in boys. I mean I know it's all biology, the old primordial ooze and doing our bit to make more of the species and all that, but it's never really appealed to me."

"Not something I've thought about either," said Clemency. "I mean I do love the laughs and Good Lord, the sex is fantastic but the whole baby thing, not for me thanks."

"It's not just the baby thing," said Cecilia quietly. "Can I tell you something, strictly between you and me? Swear to never tell?"

"Of course," said Clemency, "pass the cigarette, you're getting it all wet."

"I think I fancy girls."

"Ah, well, you wouldn't be the first."

"You're not shocked?"

"Why? Is that shocking?"

Cecilia ducked under the water, splashing Clemency a little, then came back up glistening. "Well, I had hoped there would be a little frisson of taboo but I keep forgetting that you've lived about ten lives by now so not much shocks you. Are you okay with it?"

"Okay?"

"With me being different?"

"Didn't we start out this conversation saying we're not like other people?"

"Well, yes." Cecelia paused, "Boys are just so prickly."

"Well, to be honest I like that, but yes I know what you mean."

"And smelly."

Clemency laughed then took a long drag on the cigarette, "Actually, Cecil has no smell; it's quite odd really. If he does, it's the drink he's had or the cigarette he's smoked and now and then... incense."

"Oh."

"But look here, this is the 20th century, love is love. There's not enough of it to worry about the direction it takes you. Well, okay, in Berlin I saw a few directions love went that I worried about but honestly to live I say, just move towards love."

"Oh I knew you'd understand."

"Just no butch hairstyles, agreed?"

"Agreed."

Clemency stretched out her legs and put her head back. Cecilia reached and took the cigarette. "Do any of your friends know?" asked Clemency.

"Good Lord no, they're all as mature as beets. I don't trust them with news like this... at least not right now."

"Okay, well, it's your birthday, let's celebrate that. Then we'll work on the future. One day at a time."

"Thank you Clem, you're wonderful."

"Now," said Clemency sitting up, "let's get you in to your birthday suit."

Cecilia stood up and laughed, "I think I already am!"

Chapter Five

Clemency found Cecil in the library reclining in a large leather chair, his feet up on an ottoman, holding a book in one hand, a glass in the other, eyes closed.

"Cecil! What number is that?"

Cecil sat bolt upright almost dropping his glass, "Darling! I swear to goodness that was number …" he paused, "two."

"Well go carefully, this is family, whatever you do will be broadcast to the entire clan. Be on your best behaviour."

"Why darling, when am I not on my best behaviour? Insults me for you to even say that." Woolley stood up then fell over the ottoman. "Damned thing! Snuck up on me like a corgi.

"Just two drinks?" Clemency said archly.

"The sea air, you know, can't feel a thing. Come, the night is young and we are young. Let's live my darling. Live!" He pulled Clemency towards him and kissed her passionately.

"Oh Woolley, I do love you."

"And I you darling." As they embraced Clemency quietly took the martini glass out of Cecil's hand and placed it on the table.

The ancient library clock chimed the hour. Cecilia burst in shouting, "Dinner is served, do come, dinner!"

Cecil smiled, "Darling, tide and time and dinner," and reluctantly they pulled themselves apart.

"Oh do come quickly," Cecilia said impatiently, "you must come and meet my friends!"

Cecil looked at Clemency and smiled, "Right. We must meet the friends. I might suggest straightening your camisole darling, your bosom is rather distracting."

"That's it, I'm putting on a sack."

"Oh please darling, never a sack."

Cecil took Clemency's arm and they followed Cecilia across the hall and into the dining room. The walls were paneled in black wood with rectangular patterns of marquetry. The enormous fireplace was made of black marble brindled with white; its mantle, also black marble, was festooned with small sculptures, obelisks and human and animal skulls. Two urns filled with bizarre purple flowers sat at each end and above the mantle, a huge, ancient mirror duskily repeated the room within it. The ceiling was vaulted and in the centre, hanging from an ornate chain, was a crystal-encrusted chandelier blazing with light. To one side of the fireplace sat an enormous grandfather clock, also of black wood, with a tarnished dial sluggishly marking the passing time that also showed moon phases and tidal changes. The floor was covered in well-worn Persian carpets and upon the walls were dark paintings of ships and mariners and the sea. Bowls of fresh cut flowers were everywhere and mixed with the fresh sea air drifting in from an open window, they created an intoxicating scent. A fire in the huge hearth tried gallantly to take off the sudden chill that had arisen and in the distance, as if the room wasn't exotic enough, a peacock cawed.

"This is such a beautiful room," said Clemency.

"Beautiful," sighed Cecil, looking only at her.

There were four already seated at table: two men in black tie and dinner jackets, their hair slicked back and glistening, and two elongated and elegant girls dressed beau monde in shimmering almost translucent shifts.

"Come you two!" said Cecilia grabbing Clemency and Cecil. "Come and meet the gang. This rather odd looking chap with the monocle is Freddy." She said, pointing to the rat-like young man on her left.

"How do you do," said Freddy, snapping his head in a bow.

"And the rather fetching creature with him is Jing-Wei."

"Charmed," Jing-Wei demurred.

"And this brute here is Chas. Chas plays rugby at school, can you imagine, disporting himself hither and yon like a savage!"

"Cut it out Cece. It's perfectly natural for chaps to be involved in team sports. I am also president of the chess club." He stood, extending a hand, "Nice to meet you both."

"Oh, I do apologize!" laughed Cecilia, kissing him on the cheek. "And this ravishing creature is Fiona. Fiona already has two love ballads and one artist's suicide to her credit."

"Heavens!" exclaimed Woolley.

Fiona sighed, "Oh Cece, must you always bring that up?"

"Fiona is from Canada, but we won't hold that against her, she is simply fascinating." Cecilia took her hand and kissed it.

"I say," Chas chimed in, "I thought we were in France not the bally Island of Lesbos!"

The group erupted in a collective "boo" and threw breadsticks at Chas.

"For heaven's sakes, I was only joshing!" said Chas waving off the onslaught of crust.

Cecil smiled charmingly, "Well, I am Cecil Herbert Woolley, double "U" double 'O' double 'L' E-Y, I am … shakes … what am I Clemency?"

Clemency smiled, "Tipsy?"

"I am nothing of the sort. I am quite, quite sober and I am, as best as I can describe it, a… consulting detective."

"Oh how fascinating," Jing-Wei purred.

Cecilia turned to Clemency and finished the introductions, "And this is my absolute favourite cousin, Clemency de la Tour."

"How lovely to meet you all,' said Clemency with a smile. "But where is everyone else? When we arrived the staff were setting up for what looked like a great horde but here we are only seven."

Cecilia pulled Clemency over to the table, "Oh, they're coming later. As I do not officially turn 21 until 10:59 this evening, I decided to start the great bash then. This is dinner for the smart set, my closest and dearest."

"Here, here," toasted Chas.

"We are honoured," said Cecil, clicking his heals, "to

be counted as a member of the smart set. Ah ... where would you like us to sit?"

"Oh! Well we have a bit of a muddle, don't we? With an uneven number, I would really like you and Cecil to sit at the ends, pater and mater like but this table is so enormous you'd be miles away so you can both wriggle in beside me."

"Hattie isn't coming?" asked Clemency.

"Oh no," said Cecelia.

"She wouldn't eat with the likes of us, the spawn of decadent capitalistic swine," sneered Chas. "She's eating gruel and dried bread somewhere."

"Chas!"

"Dislikes us all on principle it seems," continued Freddy in a faint reedy voice. "Typical of that sort to generalize. Suits their dogma."

"She's a kooky old bird," said Chas, "but I like her ... even if she has no time for me."

A door opened and a butler came over to Cecilia, "Madam, shall we serve the soup?"

"Yes, Fitch, that would be lovely. Places everyone, soup!"

Three similarly dressed footmen came out from behind a screen, two carrying wine in ornate glass decanters and one an enormous silver soup tureen. A white-gloved hand, holding the matching serving spoon, displaced a delicious green swirl of soup into Cecilia's bowl. "Cream of asparagus," she said, "cook's spécialité de la maison!"

"Makes your pee smell something awful!" cracked Chas as everyone booed and threw more bread sticks at him.

"Look you crowd, if you're going to throw bread at me every time I open my gob I'm going to stay silent for the rest of the meal."

"Is that a promise?" said Freddy, polishing his monocle.

Chas pointed a finger, "Now look here old man…"

"Boys!" Cecilia clapped her hands. "Love! It's my birthday."

"Well, it does make it pungent," grumbled Chas.

"Quite right," Cecil said, picking up his glass of wine and sniffing. "Asparagusic acid, as the name implies, is found only in asparagus. As our bodies digest the asparagus plant it breaks down the asparagusic acid into a group of related sulfur-containing compounds such as, well, for example dimethyl sulfide, a compound similar to that found in garlic, the spray of a skunk or odorized natural gas; in other words compounds containing molecules which give off a rather unpleasant scent."

"Darling," Clemency said, trying with her eyes to imply he'd said enough.

Cecil put up a finger, "Now these molecules also share another key characteristic, that is they're volatile, they have a low enough boiling point that they can vaporize and enter a gaseous, rather scented state at room temperature."

Clemency put down her soupspoon, "Darling, please."

"Asparagusic acid, on the other hand, is not volatile so the asparagus plant itself does not have an odour. However, once eaten, once the stomachs digestive juices set to work, the acid becomes volatile and creates rummy, sulphur-bearing compounds. And so, as Chas so astutely pointed out, once peed out and exposed to oxygen the molecules boil and release quite an aromatic scent. Why in 1781, Benjamin Franklin wrote a letter to the Royal Academy…"

"Darling!" Clemency shouted, "Eat your soup."

Chapter Six

Once dinner was finished the women moved to the library to play the gramophone while the men remained seated around the dining table drinking port.

"Are we really sitting here drinking port with the women in the other room?" sighed Freddy.

"Appears so," said Chas pounding back his drink and pouring another then passing the decanter. "How long do you suppose we have to sit here? I'd rather be with the women folk."

Cecil slowly sipped his port. The glass was cut crystal, something he was not fond of though he did enjoy the play of light in and around the glass. The port however, the port was delectable. He rolled it around inside the goblet, holding it up to the light, a beautiful tawny brown. Could this be a Muscat 1896? How is that even possible? What a lovely, thick grapey taste. Like drinking a raisin, no, like…

Chas coughed, "I suspect Cecilia isn't playing for the other side."

"What does that mean?" said Freddy, pouring another glass.

…slipping down a slope of soft velvet. Surely this is

Italian Muscat, could it be even pre-phylloxera…

"I've done more than a man's share of trying to get her attention, she's a right comely girl," Chas finished his port and reached across the table for the decanter, "and nothing. Not a bat-squeak of interest."

Freddy polished his monocle, "Did it ever occur to you that it might be just you she is not interested in and not the entire male sex?"

"Impossible, how could someone not want me?" he said without a touch of irony, "Besides, you've seen how she looks at Fiona, those huge cow eyes. Unnerving is what it is."

…Reminds me of that time with Clemency, when was that '25, '26? Rented a barge. Rarely out of bed before 11…

"I say Cecil," bellowed Chas, "what's your take on all this?"

"Wha… what?" Cecil stuttered, shocked back into the moment.

"Cecilia. Not playing for the right side, tipping the old velvet if you get my meaning."

"Good Lord Chas, why is it a concern of yours?"

"I fancy her. Chap's got a right to fancy someone. It's the war, made women think they could be anything they pleased."

"Oh for heaven's sake," cried Freddy.

Suddenly an incredible din was heard throughout the house. Chas jumped up, ready for action, "What's that? Sounds like a fire bell."

Cecilia burst into the room, "Come you men, a storm's come up since we've been gorging, hardly noticed it while dining, but a ship is out there being blown straight for the rocks. Grab a mackintosh quick, we've got to help!"

The men ran into the hall, now wide-awake and adrenaline sober. The clamour of the bell was deafening. They found Hattie in the entrance shouting instructions.

"We've sent word to the other guests not to come, the sea swell is enormous. You lot, here, take a coat, any of you know how to row?"

Chas stepped forward, "I stroked for Oxford," he placed a hand on his heart, "Horsfall himself wept at my skill!"

"Good man," said Hattie, slapping him hard. "You three then, follow the men down to the shore, there's a skiff tied down there, we may have to rescue! Hurry now, hurry!"

Cecilia came running in with Clemency, Fiona and Jing-Wei, "Mother what can we do?!"

"Get up to the tower and man the light; if they don't know the sea 'round here they'll surely fetch up on the rocks."

"Right!" shouted Cecilia. "Come on girls!"

Cecil stood back, still holding his glass of port. He slowly sipped the last of the drink and let it drift burning a delicious lyrical footpath down his throat. He smiled then placed the glass safely on the table and grabbed an old mackintosh hung by the door and followed the rest out of the house.

He was instantly slapped in the face by icy sea air. It pushed him back, piercing in its intensity; it was now blowing at full gale force. He was perplexed; why hadn't they noticed the change during dinner? The light was preternatural, a bottle glass green giving everything an unearthly glow. He made his way around the house and watched as the other two, bent against the wind, slowly made their way towards the stairs down the cliff to the ocean side dock. The trees at the edge of the lawn bent and twisted and shook. The air smelled of salt and ozone. He looked out to the ocean; in the strange light he could see the ship, tilting in the wind, a black shape on the undulating horizon. He started out but halfway to the cliff stairs remembered Clemency's tale of the cave where boats could moor. An idea struck; if he could place a flare on each side to mark the sheltered cave, with any luck the ship could steer away from the rocks and towards the light and safety. He started back towards the house. It felt like forever crossing the slick lawn, pushing his way against the wind. The only sound was the roar of the gale. When he finally reached the house he was drenched and exhausted.

"Hattie!" he cried. "Where is the rescue kit, I will need light!"

Chapter Seven

Cecil made his way down the twisting set of stairs, armed only with a torch and a handful of flares. The torch gave off little light but he knew he must be getting close to the sea as the stairs were becoming slick with moisture and he could hear the dull roar of the wind. He came to a small rusted door and taking out the key Hattie had given him, inserted it in the lock; the door creaked open revealing a large antechamber with an entrance to a passageway he hoped led to the cave.

The door slammed shut behind him with such a great violence it made him drop the torch in surprise. His heart sank as he heard it clacker down the stone stairs of the passageway. In desperation he pulled out one of the flares and struck the cap; it spluttered then ignited, illuminating the crags of the rock face, practically blinding him in the process. When his eyes adjusted, he continued down the slick steps and finally into the cave. He could see why this would be a pirate's paradise, the space was enormous with an entrance opening large enough to let the tallest galleon pass untouched.

The noise that came from the boiling sea was tremendous; it poured in, coursing violently then quickly calming as it rolled into the sheltered pool at the back with an echoed slap. Around the edge of the cave a three-foot ledge had been carved out; attached to the walls were ancient and rusted mooring rings. He quickly placed the lit flare on the ground by the opening.

Cecil then inched his way along the ledge towards the dark entrance and set off another flare, this time sheltering his eyes with his arm. It soared into life filling one side of the cave with harsh yellow light. He secured it in a gap in the rocks then edged his way along the slick walkway back. The green boiling sea sluicing in terrified him; the undertow, he thought, must be formidable.

Sensing he was running out of time, he scuttled along to the opposite side, slipping in green slime and damp sea moss. When he was parallel to the light on the other side, he knocked the cap off the flare and set it to life then made his return way along the wall, grateful for the flares' light. When he reached the back of the cave by the entrance, he ignited the second last of the flares and placed it on the ground in line with the entrance. It was certainly impressive how bright the combined flares were; he just hoped they were bright enough to catch the attention of the ship.

Woolley shuddered. There was something eerie about this grotto in the sea — instead of reflecting the light of the flares the green water of the pool seemed to absorb them.

Chapter Eight

Cecilia was perplexed and becoming desperate, "I have no idea why it won't work!"

The women had crowded into the glass observation tower at the top of the house, frantically trying to turn on the ancient brass search light, while all around them wind whipped and lightening flashed terrifyingly. Jing-Wei was holding a cigarette lighter aloft, her reflection in the glass a dot of blue flame and her illuminated face. "My father is a lighthouse keeper," she said, "may I look?"

The women stood back and let her examine the instrument. "I've never seen anything like this but I think I understand its construction. Could someone hold the lighter for me?"

Clemency took it and tried to hold it in such a way that Jing-Wei could see the workings more clearly. The storm lashed the tiny room, the howling wind whistling through the cracks, rattling the small glass panes. In the strange light, the sea was a horrible churning surface frothed with white foam. They could just make out the black silhouette of the ship headed hell-bound towards the rocks.

"I've got it!" Jing-Wei said and the lamp clacked on,

filling the room with light.

"Heavens!" shouted Fiona, "That is bright! Can you turn it? Jing, shine it on the ship!"

"No, shine it on the rocks," said Cecelia. "We'd blind the men on the ship if we turned it on them!"

With a huge effort they pushed the lamp until it pointed down towards the sea. There was a huge flash of lightening and almost instantly a report of thunder.

Fiona screamed, "Wait! I can't see it!"

Cecilia pressed her face against the glass, "What?! It was just there a second ago. It can't have gone down so fast!"

They all pressed their faces to the glass and to their horror there was no ship to be seen

Woolley was about to start back when he saw the light from a torch shinning down the passageway. Running towards it he met Chas and Freddy dashing towards him. Freddy was bellowing.

"The ship! The ship is gone!"

"What?!" Cecil shouted. "Did it hit the rocks? Are there survivors?"

Breathlessly Chas continued, "We were watching it from the dock, readying the boat as we thought for sure it was going to run aground. None of us can say when but there was a great flash of lightening and suddenly it … it…"

Freddy sounding panicked, continued, "It just wasn't there!"

"Come now, how can that be?" asked Cecil. "There must have been a mast, a flare, something, someone must have seen something!"

Freddy took his handkerchief out of his pocket and mopped his face, "Nothing…nothing…nothing," he moaned, "I was watching, keeping an eye out on its exact location when suddenly it wasn't there. It didn't go down…it didn't sink… it was just…GONE!

Woolley was about to query further when Chas, looking up, whispered, "My God, what is this place?" In their haste the boys had not noticed the enormity of the empty cave. Lit with the artificial glow of the flares, it was quite a sight. Cecil made to speak when suddenly all the flares died and they were thrust into complete and utter darkness.

"Quick, there's another flare," shouted Cecil. "Freddy, give me your torch."

"I dropped it," cried Freddy. All three men fell down on their hands and knees to search for the missing flashlight. Freddy found it and turned it on. He swept the beam of light across the pool and screamed.

"Good lord," gasped Chas.

There, resting calmly in the cave, was an enormous black yacht.

Freddy screamed and dropped the light again.

Cecil shouted, "Quick, find the torch. We need light."

Chas said, fishing in his pocket, "Wait! I have a cigarette lighter!"

"Excellent, give it here." Cecil took the slim silver box but before he could light it Freddy screamed again, "Look! Inside! A light!" They all turned, for through the grimy windows of the boat, a single shaft of light could be seen.

Cecil bawled to the ship, "Can we help?" No response. "Is anyone hurt?"

The beam of light disappeared.

Cecil leaned as forward as he dare and shouted, "I say, is there anything we can do?"

The darkness of the cave was overwhelming. After a

minute or so, the yellow beam inside the craft re-appeared nearing the outer section of the boat.

A hatch door opened and out stepped a dark figure with a gleaming white skeletal face. "Hello," he yelled, trying to be heard over the howling wind. "My name is Sacheverell, Lord Sacheverell Linquist. There are three of us here, myself, my sister and our doctor friend. We are grateful to whomever lit those torches. Can you tell us where we are? We've been sailing for days, utterly, hopelessly lost."

"Good God man," yelled back Chas. "What about your crew…charts?"

"Oh, we had crew. They … left us and none of us can read the charts."

"What? Left you?" Cecil was confounded, "Look, let's get you off this thing and onto dry land."

"What in blazes," came the voice of Aunt Hattie and suddenly the cave was awash in light. "Haven't any of you brilliant men heard of light switches? The whole island is electrified; the cave is too. What boat is this? Is this what we saw off shore?"

"Mrs. de la Tour!' shouted Chas pointing to the figure on the deck, "this is Mr. Linquist."

"Lord," said Lord Linquist.

"Lord … Linquist. We were just about to help him and the other passengers off."

"Comrade, you are welcome here. Let's get you and the others inside and dry." She said and turned to the staff that had accompanied her. "Mr. Finch, would you and Mr. Baines mind checking on the rest of the guests? Oh, and try and find the band. I hope they weren't blown away."

"M'am," said Baines and the two men returned up the passageway.

"Madam, I cannot thank you enough," shouted Lord Linquist to Hattie. "I fear much longer out at sea and we would have been goners." He bowed then turned around and called out, "Holly, Dr. Tibits, we are safe, we have found solid ground!"

Chas rushed forward, "Here, pass me the gangplank."

Lord Linquist reached down and began passing over a thin black plank. "Got it," said Chas and rested it against the ground.

While they busied themselves Cecil took in the scene before him. The Lord was rail thin, his face almost a mask with tight pale lips, above which hinted a pencil thin moustache. He was dressed all in black with a red paisley cravat that erupted in a flourish beneath his chin. The boat also was black; a large fantail flying the flag of a country Cecil could not identify. The name painted on her side was The Mircalla. Its darkened windows bubbled with moisture.

Hattie came around the side; the gangplank in place, Lord Linquist began crossing. He stopped suddenly mid-plank and placing is hand on his heart said hesitantly to Hattie, "May I come ashore?"

Hattie roared with laughter, "Sir, you are most welcome on my island, all of you."

The Lord smiled and stepped ashore.

"Holly?" he shouted back at the boat, "we are most welcome."

Slowly the hatch opened a second time, and out of

the cabin stepped the most ravishing creature Chas or Freddy had ever seen.

"I say!" gasped Chas, "Lord!" exclaimed Freddy, his monocle popping off.

"Gentlemen," said Lord Lindquist, as she stepped off the gangplank. "This is my sister Holly. Holly, this is everybody."

She turned to Cecil and in a low whisper said, "Thank you."

Cecil smiled, "Our pleasure."

"Allow me," said Chas reaching out and taking her pale, elongated hand.

Behind her a third man appeared; he was elegant, handsome and clean-shaven. He, too, was thin and like Lord Linquist of a sallow completion, with dark rings around his eyes and thin, tight lips. He was dressed in a black dinner jacket with velvet lapels, a white dress shirt and a black bow tie. The suit had a vest and a silver watch chain with a fob that hung in the pocket. This must be Dr. Tibits thought Cecil.

When on shore, the doctor took Chas' hand. "Thank you sir, thank you." He then kissed Aunt Hattie's cheek, twice on each side. "Madam. Thank you. You've saved our lives."

"Think nothing of it. These stairs lead into the house; it's warm and dry there. Come and tell us of your adventures at sea."

Lord Linquist bowed, "With pleasure madam."

Cecil hung back, watching the party as they entered the passageway leading up to the house. "Curious," he thought, rubbing his chin. "Curious."

Chapter Ten

The girls had gone upstairs to find something more practical to change into while the others settled down in the Red Room, a comfortable octagonal-shaped room at the back of the house that the family used to view the sea. Lord Linquist was admiring some Meissen birds, which were perched on the mantle while Holly and the doctor rested on one of the innumerable couches. Hattie was off looking for food and Cecil was mixing a cocktail, staring intensely at the back of the Lord.

"This is exquisite," Linquist said, picking up the delicate china bird. Turning to Cecil he asked, "Has it been in the family long?"

Cecil siphoned out a drink and said, "I'm new here myself. Up until 4 o'clock this afternoon I didn't even know this island existed."

"Really," said the Lord, setting the bird down.

"Cocktail?"

"No, I never drink ... martinis."

Professor Janek unexpectedly burst into the room. He was still in peasant dress but had added a yellow sou'wester hat to his attire. Dropping a ragged suitcase by the door he headed for one of the couches. "Is that a cocktail, I am famished!" he said, taking Cecil's drink out of his hand. He swallowed it in one go then flopped wearily into a chair.

Cecil frowned, "Would you like a cocktail dear boy?"

"Yes, double, all gin." He put his head in his hands dramatically. "Oh! Oh! That Hattie has made my brain ache and now I am trapped on her island for all eternity! Eternity!" He gestured dramatically then suddenly noticing the others, asked bluntly, "Who are these people?"

"They are guests," said Cecil, passing him a tumbler of gin.

"Guests? It is storming, how did they get here?" He turned to Lord Linquist, "How did you get here?"

"Why, by boat."

"Impossible, the storm is too great."

Cecil fixed another martini and dropped himself into an oversized red velvet armchair with gold tassels, "Nonetheless old bean, that is the manner of their arrival and there are witnesses to prove it."

"Doesn't matter," said the Professor, pounding back half his glass of gin, "I am no longer a guest and I do not care how they came. It is my leaving that I care about."

"Goodness, such drama," said the Lord languidly and fished out a delicate silver case from his jacket pocket. He took out a cigarette and lit it, flicking the match into the fire.

Holly got up and moved slowly to the bookshelf. "These are all very dull books. Are they all about economics or the repressed or by Shaw?" she whispered.

"As I said," said Cecil finishing his drink, "I'm new

here myself. I would suspect they are Hattie's. I'm lead to believe she's very left wing."

"Ha!" Professor Janek snorted into his glass, "Fascist dictator maybe." He finished his drink, "Another!"

Cecil cocked an eyebrow, "Drinks cart's over there, Professor. Please help yourself." The professor grunted but did not move.

Presently the girls came back into the room. Clemency, having only come dressed for dinner, had changed into something from Cecilia's closet; Cecil was struck by just how lovely she looked in Cecilia's black cardigan and riding pants. He smiled dreamily, "Darling, there is simply no one else."

"Cecil stop. Is that a martini? Are you the only one drinking?"

"No, no, the professor is helping me."

Professor Janek snorted.

A volley of rain thrashing against the windows in harsh, watery gusts, reminded all that the storm continued, unabated. Although the room was cozy with the fire, Cecilia hugged herself and shuddered, "Such a dreadful storm, I've never seen it so bad."

Jing-Wei said, "My parents lighthouse is in the middle of Penchia Islet in Taiwan. There, the storms there are ferocious and seem to never end."

Holly pushed a book back on to the shelf and purred, "Your parents live in a lighthouse?" "Yes, it's a very lonely existence, but we raise finches to lighten the days."

Cecilia hugged Jing-Wei, "Oh Jing, you are simply the most interesting girl in the world."

Professor Janek, who had gotten up and now was

pouring straight gin into his glass said, "I do not see that."

Fiona laughed, "Who is this horrible man?"

"Nobody," answered Cecilia and walked over to where Holly was standing. "I am Cecilia de la Tour."

Holly turned and smiled wanly. "Yes." She purred, "Thank you for giving us shelter, I so hope we haven't put you out dreadfully." She reached out and touched Cecilia on her bare arm, which raised the hairs and gave her gooseflesh. She suddenly felt a weakness in her knees; breathing became difficult.

"No, no … no trouble at all."

Holly held her with her eyes, "Well, we cannot thank you enough. You and your family have been so kind."

Chas rushed into the room, "Has anyone seen that bally band? Where did they get up to when the storm hit? Are those martinis? I could tuck myself into one of those right now!"

Freddy followed in saying worriedly, "I can't find them anywhere."

Cecil sipped his drink, "I did not see them. Did you my love?"

"No," said Clemency walking over from the drinks cart and positioning herself delicately on the arm of Cecil's chair. Cecil smiled, appreciatively patting her thigh. "Cecilia," he said, "Holly was complaining of your books."

"Not complaining," Holly demurred, "just sad that they are all so dull." Turning to Cecilia, "Surely these are not your books?"

"No, no … they're mostly Hattie's," she said nervously, "I have a small library in my room."

"Oh, I would love to see your books. Would you show me? Don't you find looking at a person's bookshelf is much the same as reading their diary? So personal, so revealing." She took Cecilia's hand passionately, "Will you show me?"

"I… I… why, yes. Now?"

"Oh yes, please."

"My room is a mess but follow me."

"What did I tell you!" grumbled Chas into his drink. "El Lesbos."

Fiona sighed, "Oh Chas, come into the 20th Century. You're such a bore."

"Bore eh? I'm not the one carrying on like this is some backroom Roman orgy."

"Have I missed something?" said Lord Lindquist

"Yes," Professor Janek added, "What am I missing here?"

Chapter Eleven

Enormous bursts of thunder shook the house while lightening cast fantastic shadows on the walls. Holly grabbed Cecilia's hand as she led them up the stairs and down the hall to her room.

"I love your house," said Holly in a whisper. "It is the perfect place for a ghost story. The house is so foreboding, the air is so charged."

"The house has quite a history so it's small wonder you feel that way."

"Really? How interesting." Holly was still holding Cecilia's hand, her grip firm, her hand icy cold.

"This is my room," said Cecilia opening the door, "I'm afraid it's a bit of a mess." Holly smiled enigmatically and went in. The room was dark but for a fire blazing in the hearth. There was just enough light for Holly to make out a sizable, oddly-shaped room stuffed with arm chairs, bureaus, pillows and books; a large four-poster bed was set against the far wall and to its right, an alcove window with a window seat covered in pillows. Cecilia tried to tidy but Holly stopped her. "No, please. My room is much the same though not as comfortable or as romantic. Oh, I could fall in love in this room." She pulled Cecilia close. "Have you ever?"

"Ever what?"

"Fallen in love in this room." Holly closed her eyes as if swooning, then opened slowly. "Oh! Are these all your books?"

Holly's intensity made Cecilia feel nervous and awkward. "Yes, mostly. I mean I've taken some from the library downstairs but essentially they are all mine. I bring boxes of them when we come as I so love to read."

"So do I," she whispered and picked up a book that was resting open on the arm of the chair nearest. "Ruskin. Really?"

Cecilia felt defensive, "I keep trying to read him. I keep thinking I should like him more."

"I agree with you. I did enjoy The Stones of Venice; you must have read that? So wonderful."

"I feel ashamed to say I haven't read it."

"You MUST. Better still, have you been? If not, you MUST go to Venice.

Cecilia shook her head.

"Oh Cecilia, I will take you!" Holly dropped the book to the ground and put out her arms. "The canals by moonlight, the sound of the water lapping on the ancient stone. Oh, it is so marvellous! The buildings. The palazzos. We have a Great Aunt there and her palace faces the Grand Canal. I cannot tell you what it is like to just stand there as if you are taking part in its ancient history. To be able to look out at the black water and the blacker sky and see all the stars. The stars! Oh, and the sounds of the people, the music in the midnight cafes. That lovely

Italian they speak there…" Holly stopped becoming suddenly self-aware. She reached out and took both Cecilia's hands, pulling her to the window seat; she had a gentle smell of dry earth. They looked out the window together. Holly shivered, "The storm is worsening but I feel so safe here." She put her arm around Cecilia and leaning forward gently kissed her on the cheek.

"Oh," said Cecilia, "I wasn't expecting that."

"I'm sorry. Did I go too far?"

"No, I liked it. It's just we're English and English people don't do things like that."

"Like what?"

"Kiss. Touch. Anything really."

Holly leaned over and kissed Cecilia on the lips. It was the gentlest of sensations, like velvet. "Is that okay?"

"More than okay, I think I may burst."

A huge clap of thunder rattled the window and the girls squealed then started laughing. Cecilia played with the curtain, "I would so love to travel more. I have only gone with Momma and that's mostly been to communist conventions. Nothing romantic, everything just grey, grey, grey."

Holly took Cecilia's hand, they were sitting very close, their legs touching, "I've been to so many places I've almost forgotten where; Brussels and Bruges, Bath, Bulgaria, all over China, Japan. I've been to India and Nepal, Singapore and Taiwan, Scandinavia, Iceland."

"What is it like?"

"What is what like?"

"To be free."

Holly let go of Cecilia and said bitterly, "I'm not free."

Confused, Cecilia took back Holly's hand. "I'm sorry. Did I say something wrong?"

Holy turned away, "No, no, it's me," she put her finger on the cold window. "I can just hit the ground sometimes. Emotionally. I feel as light as air when I meet someone as magical and lovely as you — charged and ecstatic. But then reality pricks me like a thorn and I fall." She paused. "I have a city inside of me, this made up place where I wander and feel safe. I live there, in that city. It's full of all the things I wish that were; shop windows warmly lit and filled with books, twisty winding streets, magic shops and parks, parks at night. And bridges. Then someone says something, or something ugly happens around me and my magical city disappears and I feel cold and hollow, like a bird who's flown into a window."

"Oh, I'm so sorry Holly. What did I say? Please!"

"It's not you. How could you know? It's just I'm not free, Cecilia."

"I'm sorry, I don't understand."

Holly got up and began to pace the room, "I'm not free like you think. I am trapped. You are so lucky. You have this house, your life. You can come and go. My life is shadows. Rules. Death." Holly walked over and violently took Cecilia arms. "Look at me, what do you see?"

"Holly, you're hurting me."

"What do you see? Answer me!" Holly let go of Cecilia and ran over to the dressing table and grabbed a mirror. She ran back, pushing herself beside Cecilia. "Look! Look at us in the mirror. This is my life. This is what I see!"

To Cecilia's horror there was only one face reflected in mirror, her own; Holly was nowhere to be seen. She began to scream. "No, it can't be! No."

"I am a vampire Cecilia. I am here to kill you!"

"It can't be, it can't be! There is no such thing as vampires! It's only a book, a fiction. They don't really exist."

"Don't they? Oh how I wish that were true."

Confused, Cecilia started to weep uncontrollably. Holly gently touched her hand, "Why are you crying?"

"Because … because I am falling in love with you."

It was Holly's turn to burst into tears.

A knock came on the door; it opened slightly. It was Cecil. "Everything okay? I heard unsettling noises."

Cecilia grabbed a handkerchief and dabbed her eyes. "Come in Cousin Cecil."

"Cousin Cecil, hmm, not sure I like the sound of that. I came up to say that Hattie's rustled up some grub for the shipwrecked few. Want to come join us?"

Cecilia loudly blew her nose. Holly took the handkerchief and did the same.

Cecil frowned, "Can't be all that bad. Is there anything I can do to make things better?"

"Oh Cecil, if you only knew…"

Cecil crossed the floor and took Cecilia in his arms, "There, there my pet. Holly, have you been …" It was then that he saw, or to be precise didn't see Holly's reflection in the mirror. "Oh Good Lord." He jumped back and pointing a finger at Holly shouted, "I knew I felt something queer about you. Vampire!" He backed away slowly, crossing to fingers into a crucifix, "And the rest?"

Holly blew her nose again and whispered, "All. We are all vampires."

Cecilia again burst into tears.

Cecil fished for a cigarette. "Well, that adds an interesting twist to an already interesting, and for me, far too twisted evening. May I ask, was your arrival intentional?"

Holly looked up, "I think so... yes. We've been travelling along the coast for some time, moving from place to place. Father is on some sort of quest. We can go for months, years even without feeding but Father is gorging. I think he has something in mind. I think it's becoming dangerous for us ... for our kind ... and he wants to hide us away."

"Ah," Cecil lit his cigarette and exhaled. "You will understand if I insist that there will be no blood sucking shenanigans here tonight."

Holly shivered then said quietly, "I'm sick of death."

"Yes, well, we will have to have a talk."

"What are you going to do?" said Holly, panicked. "You can't expose us. Surely that would cause alarm and if anyone tried to do anything ... Mr. Woolley, you must never underestimate our strength, our ... power."

"Oh Cecil, can't we just act like we didn't know?" Cecilia said, walking over to Holly and taking her hand.

"Cecilia," Cecil said earnestly, "Holly is a vampire. She is a predator, a killer. She is ancient and she is dangerous."

"Uncle Cecil... please... don't force her to leave...not now," she said then turned and brushed her hand against Holly's cheek.

Cecil looked at Holly.

"This is not of my doing," she said.

Cecil sighed. "Well, then, this is a pickle."

Holly let Cecilia go. "Mr. Woolley, we have fed enough. Fed enough to last the night, to last 50 years really. Can we not just be granted shelter and tomorrow evening we will leave?"

"How can I trust you?"

"Cecil!" cried Cecilia.

"Look here. I've known a vampire or two in my day and forgive me, their lot is worse than hop-heads or opium smokers." He turned to Holly, "I'm all for 'live and let live'… Lord knows I have a few quirks myself but you're liars and cheats. What you have is the supreme addiction and with it comes death, too much death. I hate it, I'm sick of it and I will not allow it here!"

"You have my word," said Holly quietly.

"Not good enough."

"What is then?"

"I want all of your words."

"Oh, if father finds out that I've told you he will be outraged."

Cecil flicked his cigarette into the fire. "There isn't any other option. We need to have a family meeting, your family that is. Get your father and that doctor… is he a doctor?"

Holly sighed, "He was, is… he was certified some time ago, his license might be expired."

"Well, 'round them up in the library. Let's get this out and see what kind of compromise we can reach."

Holly, dejected, moved silently out of the room. With her gone Cecilia suddenly felt empty. She walked over to Cecil and put her arms around him. He ran his hands through her hair, "Poor old thing. Love is funny, isn't it? Here you find love's true light and it shines out of a reanimated corpse."

"Oh Cecil, that's a horrible thing to say!"

"It's the truth my little one and you must get it into your head. No matter how lovely she is, how fascinating — and believe me the vampires I knew were a fascinating lot — you have to remember first and foremost that they are killers, predators, they will snap. Snap at the first whiff of blood, at the first hint of fear, and then where are you? Under the sod… under the sod, head chopped off, mouth stuffed with garlic, stake in the heart."

Cecilia held Cecil tightly and wept, "Oh Cecil, how horrid…"

"There, there. Come. Let's talk to them. We'll see what we can do. Maybe you and she can become pen pals or some such thing."

Chapter Twelve

"Darling," said Cecil mixing a drink in the library.

"Yes dear?" said Clemency, distractedly flipping through a *Tatler*.

"If we survive this night I am going to do something good for humanity."

Clemency stopped flipping. "Is there anything I need to know about? The last time you said something like that we were almost attacked by some monstrous being that resembled a radish."

"No, nothing so brassicaceae, however darling, things have gotten a little more complicated." Cecil poured clear liquid into a glass and holding his hand up, sipped.

"More complicated? More complicated? Darling, how could things become more complicated? We are stranded on an island in the middle of a horrendous storm; a ship floundered almost killing its passengers; we are surround by youth and communists and relatives… more complicated?"

Cecil smiled. "Darling when you get angry, you get the most delicious red splotches on your cheeks. They really are adorable."

"Cecil!" Clemency chastised. "Focus! What is going on?!"

"Well darling…" Cecil began to shake another drink; the last had too much vermouth, perhaps a dirty martini…

"Cecil! Focus!"

"I am darling, I am. Complicated." He poured his drink and then, glass in hand, walked over to the library door and closed it. "Darling, the three we rescued from their watery demise are not what they seem."

"What?"

"They are not human as we know it. They are… dead. Well, not dead…were once dead…. briefly."

"What are you talking about?"

"They are the Undead… Nosferatu… Vampire."

"That's it! You are cut off. You've drunk far too much tonight."

"Darling, I am not drunk nor am I pulling your leg. That Holly girl confessed as much to Cecilia. And she had no reflection…in the mirror…not there. This is all really very grave." Cecil chortled, "Grave."

"Hand me your drink."

Cecil stepped back and in one swallow downed it. "Darling," he said, suddenly very serious. "This is not a problem of alcohol! This is much worse; this is blood lust! Evil! The power of darkness incarnate. The undead! I've called a family meeting… Holly's family."

Clemency shivered then frowned, "They're all vampires?"

"To the last drop. Now, as a gentleman, I believe that they should not be cast out into the night with the storm raging. At the same time I will not allow these bloodsuckers to harm the love of my life…"

"So sweet."

"…or her family." Cecil walked over to the window and pulled the curtain back. "This storm has not let up one jot. Mother Nature must certainly be angry at someone."

There came a knock at the door. Cecil looked at Clemency, "Ah, the uninvited guests. Come in!" he shouted.

Holly entered first looking ghastly pale, her face stained with blood-tinted tears. Next came Lord Linquist then the doctor. "Ah, come in.' said Woolley. "I'd offer you a drink but I know it would be moot, you being a vampire and all."

Lord Linquist rushed for Cecil. "Father!" Holly screamed, "Remember what I said. He's on our side."

"Not necessarily 'on' your side," said Cecil. "More aware of it and here to make sure we all remain on our agreed upon, er, sides."

Lord Linquist straightened his clothes, "Sir, Holly has spoken with me and I appreciate you giving us a berth for the night, and for not … exposing us for what we are."

The doctor hissed, "Sashi, we are wasting our time. We can rip these mortals to pieces — I for one would quite enjoy myself. We can then wait out the storm and be gone before anyone's the wiser."

"No Phillip, that's not how it's done. We have been granted sanctuary. Mr. Woolley, Holly has led me to understand that we have an agreement?"

"Yes, you will be granted shelter for the night…"

"Day."

"Day. And when the storm subsides you will leave

this place and bother it no more. Is that fair?"

"Admirably."

"Then do we have an understanding?"

Lord Linquist put out his hand. Cecil smiled and took it in his. They shook. "Clemency, see, honour matters, even beyond the grave."

The doctor growled, "This is ridiculous; we've already gone back on the bargain even before it was struck."

"What!?"

"That fat professor," the doctor said flatly. "He irritated me. Now all I can taste is garlic."

Clemency gasped.

Cecil took her into his arms then turned to the doctor. "Now see here, irritating or not, he was a life; we will have none of that!"

The doctor looked at Cecil bemusedly, "Too late."

"Well," said Cecil coldly, "There will be no more of that."

Lord Linquist walked over and patted Cecil on the back. "Old habits I'm afraid but you have my word there will be no other … incidents."

"Yes, well, your word so far has…"

"My word Mr. Woolley!" said Lord Linquist strongly. He motioned for Dr. Tibits to come over and shake Woolley's hand as well. "No more incidents," agreed Tibits.

"Now," said Lindquist, "How shall we pass the evening? We are here for the night, the storm rages on, were you not about to sit down to a late night repast?"

Hattie burst into the room, "There you all are, what's going on in here, planning a revolt? There's some cold food laid out on the sideboard in the dining room. I think we all need a little sustenance after what we've been through tonight. Come on you all, come join us."

Cecil looked at Holly and her family, "Shall we?"

The Lord stepped forward and took Holly in his arms, comforting her, "Yes, a little repast would do us all a world of good. Come Doctor, come into the light."

Cecil walked over and took Clemency's arm, "Darling, if we survive this night, along with doing good, I think I should make a respectable woman out of you."

"Cecil! Sounds dreadful! And I wasn't aware I was unrespectable."

"Let's just see if we get through the night first, then we'll talk respectability."

"Oh Cecil," Clemency said, "I do love you, you know."

"It's my boyish good looks I suspect."

"And your moustache."

"But I haven't a moustache darling."

"Oh, yes, right, you haven't."

Cecil lovingly kissed her. "Come darling, let's belly up to the trough."

Arm in arm they crossed the hall and entered the dining room. The fire was re-lit and the room was aglow with electric light. Cecil was pleased that they were not too bright so as to remove entirely the shadows in the corners. The weekend party guests were already there, informally standing around holding their plates and chatting.

Freddy looked up when they entered, "Have you seen the professor?"

"What?" said Hattie, her mouth full of bun. "He's missing? Best thing he could do, the turncoat."

Jing-Wei sipped her wine and said, "He was with us in the library. He had packed his suitcase but there was no place to go in this storm."

"Yes, well," Hattie began, "He's probably off sulking somewhere. Maybe when it becomes light we'll have a quick look round the island. We should also count the silverware!"

"Momma, that's not very compassionate," said Cecilia.

"Darling, after what that man said it's a wonder I haven't ordered a firing squad myself."

Cecil laughed nervously making eye contact with Clemency. The two went over to the sideboard to contemplate the cold supper — meats, breads and fruit, some cheeses. Cecilia was standing by the fire and Holly came over and took her arm. "Thank you for this, for keeping us safe." Cecilia felt weak at her closeness, the whispered tone of Holly's voice. She found it hard to reply but finally stammered, "It was the decent thing, and my pleasure."

Holly looked at her, "I hope it remains a pleasure, I fear we've become somewhat of a burden."

"No, no burden at all." Cecilia felt she was about to faint.

Chas burst in, "See here, what are you two cooing about? Any deviled ham left?"

Holly broke into a laugh and Cecilia joined in. Chas looked at them confusedly and mumbled, "Bally Saffos-in-training."

They laughed louder. Chas gave them a cold stare.

Cecil was filling his plate. "What a crowd of misfits. Wasn't expecting an evening quite like this."

Clemency, holding a plate of fruit and cheese hung onto his arm like a schoolgirl. "You never know what you'll get with my family," she said, popping a grape into her mouth. "Soup to nuts."

"Heavy on the nuts I'd say."

Freddie approached, screwing in his monocle. "Mr. Woolley, may I ask you something quite serious?"

"By all means Freddie."

"You were in the war, correct?"

"I was. The air force, R. A. F." he spelled out.

"And that is the nature of my question. I am presently in fourth year physics. See, I understand the idea of an aeroplane, the drag, the glide, but there's one fundamental question that's baffled me since I saw my first plane when I was young."

"And what's that?"

"How do they get off the ground?"

Cecil, realizing Freddie was bone serious, started looking for the drinks cart.

Chapter Thirteen

Holly was staring at the place settings. She turned to Cecilia and said, "This is porcelain, mid-18th century. Kaolin. It wasn't until the mid-1700s that Europeans knew how porcelain was made and stopped thinking the Chinese were magicians."

Cecilia looked down at the plates, "You seem to know a lot about plates."

"One learns a lot from spending an eternity staring at empty dishes."

"Will you show me your ship?"

"What?"

"I want to see your yacht, your room, your cabin. I want you to give me a tour. You've seen my room, I want to see yours."

Holly looked at her, "It's really not much, considering we spend so much time on it. I've become quite a minimalist over the years. Time seems to erase so much, makes things seem useless. I tried to keep mementos, little bits to remind me of pleasanter times, but they became less and less frequent, making the memory of happier times more and more like painful jabs."

"I so envy your life"

Holly silently laughed, "Envy? What do you envy about it?"

"You have all eternity to… read, to …"

Holly grabbed Cecilia's hand, "Come, I will show you my room." She pulled Cecilia violently towards the door. Cecil looked up from his drink and said firmly, "Holly, remember our agreement."

Holly stopped then laughed. "Don't worry Mr. Woolley, I'm just showing Cecilia my room, we'll be good girls and leave the door open."

Lord Linquist looked up but did not stop his conversation with Fiona. Holly caught his gaze and nodded as if acknowledging some unsaid command then pulled Cecilia out of the room and towards the passage to the grotto cave where the boat was moored.

"What was that about?" asked Cecilia.

"He told me to not kill you."

"What? I didn't hear anything said."

"No, we don't have to speak aloud to understand," Holly said, without further explanation.

As they rushed forward Cecilia was struck again by just how lovely Holly was, especially in the dim light of the hall; her chin and jaw so defined, her skin like very milky tea, her green eyes almost glowing bright in the darkness. Holly opened the door to the stairwell and immediately they were hit with a rush of frigid sea air and the distant roar of the still raging storm. She pushed on the lights. Cecilia grabbed hold of the rusty railing, "We should be careful, these steps are treacherous. It's so cold…"

Holly took off her shawl and wrapped it around

Cecilia, a simple kind gesture. The fabric was surprisingly cool and smelled of something earthy and familiar. "Oh, thank you."

"Black becomes you, it brings out your pallor."

"Um?"

"It is a compliment. Come, I want to show you."

The storm roared in the cave as the girls moved down the slick stairwell, gripping the railing to keep their footing on the wet stone. They found the boat as they had left it, laying in the sheltered harbour, its stillness betraying the harsh winds outside, its gleaming black hull looming in the light cast by the bare bulbs. Holly went first. "Give me your hand," she said reaching out to Cecilia, who tentatively placed her foot on the wooden plank. She slipped and almost fell but was caught effortlessly by Holly who said, "Almost lost you," and then impulsively kissed her.

"Oh!" said Cecilia.

"I'm sorry," said Holly and let her go.

"No, please, Holly, I've been hoping for that since you held my hand," and completely against her English nature, threw herself into Holly's arms and kissed her so passionately their teeth hit.

"Ow!" said Holly.

"I'm sorry," Cecilia said stepping back confused by hers actions.

"And I've been waiting for you to do that all night." Holly took Cecilia's hand, "Come, let me show you what I call home." As they walked, Cecilia tasted blood in her mouth.

The deck was slippery and both of the girls had difficulty

walking on the gleaming teak. Fortunately the aft deck was small and after only a few steps they were under a canopy, which sheltered an entrance. "This is the door to the main sitting room," Holly said, "We start our tour here." She pushed the door and they stepped into a darkened room. There was a palatable scent of incense and dust, thick and overpowering.

"Very dark," said Cecilia.

"Funny how suddenly I'm aware of my surroundings when they are seen through someone else's eyes," Holly said sounding almost self-conscious .

"Really…I can't see anything at all."

"Oh, I so apologize, I forgot, you're not … one of us." Cecilia felt a sad pang. "Wait, there is a lamp, let me light it." Holly lit a match, moving the flame to the wick of a glass lantern — the room was suddenly aglow in amber. Cecilia gasped at the opulence of the space. Everything was draped in velvet: the chairs, the cushions, everything in a rich black and all edged with gold piping and tassels. The room was heavily panelled in dark oak, the carpets thick and ornately patterned. There was a fireplace with a grate to contain the flames. On the walls were paintings of eerie landscapes. Books were scattered everywhere, on the floor a knocked over game of scrabble. A bar ran along one side with a mirrored back, but there were no bottles on the racks, no glasses on the shelves. "Oh Holly, I love this room."

"Do you? I guess it's nice, I am so used to it. It is comfortable, and we do spend a lot of time here. Come, follow me." Holly picked up the lantern and walked towards a door by the fireplace. It was also of dark wood and had a brass porthole; a small brass plaque was affixed just below that said 'mermaids'

They entered a long dark hall with numerous doors on either side with wall sconces dotted in between. Above, an arched glass and metal skylight ran the length of the passage; its thick glass turning what little light there was to that of a fish bowl. It was surreal and oddly calming. Each of the doors had a brass number plate and Cecilia noted that the doors were numbered indiscriminately. "This is mine." Holly said smiling. "We just put lucky numbers on the doors."

"Lucky?"

"Yes, occultually luck, if there is such a word. Mine is 13. I feel nervous showing it to you, I've shown it to no one before." Holly reached around Cecilia and pulling out a small brass key from a pocket in the shawl, inserted it into the ornate lock. There was a small click and the door swung open. The ceiling was the same arched glass as the passageway. The walls were dark purple, the floor black wood. There was nothing in the room except for a small framed engraving on the wall, a child-sized chest of drawers, a Vuitton travelling case and on the floor, an enormous black coffin.

"Oh my God!" cried Cecilia.

"Yes, that part of the legend is true though I could just as much sleep in the closet."

"Sorry…I just… wasn't expecting it. I don't know what I was expecting."

Holly gentle pushed Cecilia into the room. "Here, I want to show you something." She walked over to the engraving. "It's by an artist called Aubrey Beardsley. Have

you heard of him? He died years ago, I knew his sister...
once."

Cecilia could just make out a delicate line drawing of
a girl nude but for stripy stockings, standing erect, her left
leg tied to a post by a ribbon. "Oh ... this is beautiful."

"It's me."

Chapter Fourteen

Woolley flopped down on the bed beside Clemency. "Old thing, I'm tired."

Clemency yawned, "I could sleep past my funeral."

Woolley smiled and kissed her, "Nightcap?"

"Cecil, honestly, I think you've had enough."

Woolley frowned, "That's not the kind of thing one's own beloved says after a day like today. Besides, I've hardly consumed a thing, been too busy saving lives and brokering deals with the undead. If I may say so, I think I deserve a drink. Two even."

"Cecil, you'll be pickled before you're 40."

"But like the briny pickle, I'll live forever."

"More like something swimming in a jar of cloudy formaldehyde... the old severed ear of a criminal or..." Suddenly the air was punctured by a horrific scream.

"Good Lord!" said Woolley.

Clemency grabbed his arm, "That was nearby."

"Too nearby darling." Woolley sprang up and raced to the door. "You stay here, this could be dangerous."

"It could be more dangerous for me to stay! I'm coming with you."

Woolley frowned but knowing he could not stop her, grabbed her hand and together they ran down the hall towards where they thought the sound had emanated.

The house had come alive with shouts and the sound of footfalls. "Here!" said Chas, rounding the corner almost straight into Woolley, "You heard it too then? The scream? Couldn't place the voice, one of the girls though."

Jing-Wei ran to meet them, " I heard it too. It's Fiona. She's in the room at the far end."

Quick!" said Woolley, who sprinted off down the hall with the girls and Chas in quick pursuit.

Another blood curdling scream.

Woolley got to the room just as the door began to open. Chas stopped behind him and assumed a boxing position, ready to knock out whoever came through.

Professor Janek stumbled out, looking befuddled, covered in dried blood. "Sorry, wrong room."

Woolley was confused. Didn't the doctor confess earlier that evening that he had killed the professor?

Janek was mumbling, "I feel odd... very odd. Passed out then I woke up and was so thirsty. I'm not sure how I got into this room but I saw a glass of water by the side of the bed. I rushed to drink it but it tasted horrible. Horrible. I was still so thirsty. Then I saw the girl. Her veins seem to pop out... glowing... her blood...suddenly in my head... it's her blood I need. I don't remember... I reached over... slipped... fell on her. There was screaming... she screamed at me... I wanted her to stop."

Fiona appeared in her dressing gown visibly shaking. "That man tried to attack me!" Clemency took her in her arms.

There was a shuffle in the hall and around the corner came Hattie in a long nightgown and a man's sleeping cap, "What in blazes is going on, who screamed?! Clemency?"

"It was Fiona. The Professor wandered into the wrong room and scared her."

"Wandered, Ha! We can now add moral depravity to your long list of faults!"

The professor, still completely confused, put his arms out, "No… no. I don't know."

"You bloodsucker," hissed Jing-Wie.

"Bloodsucker?" said the professor as he reached up to feel a wound on his neck.

Aunt Hattie snorted, "That, my dear professor, has never been doubted."

Woolley sighed, "No, Hattie, he means it literally. Can we all go down to the Library, I think I need to explain a thing or …"

Then Lord Linquist appeared, still in his evening attire, holding a book. "I heard a scream but got lost trying to find my way." Seeing Fiona and the Professor, "Oh dear, has Tibits overreached himself?"

Hattie frowned, "Will someone tell me what is going on?"

Woolley took her arm, "I will. Hattie, Linquist, everyone, let's go down to the Library. Jing-Wei, can you get Cecilia and Holly? Chas, have you seen Freddy?"

"Not since we kipped. I'll go rouse him. He always could sleep through a rumpus."

Everyone milled about in the library, as no one wanted to sit. Lord Lindquist stood to one side, the professor stood nearby still looking confused. A few lights had been turned on and though the fire was almost out, the room was remarkably warm. Outside, the storm continued unabated. Eventually Jing-Wei came in looking distraught, "I've looked everywhere, I can't find Holly or Cecilia."

Chas snorted, "Lesbo tryst by the sounds of it. Damned if they don't get all the luck. Leaves us chaps out in the cold with the leapers and the dipsos."

"Chas!" hushed Jing-Wei, "You should know better. Where's Freddie?"

"Just calling it as I see it, damn it all. Freddie's on his way down, lost his monocle or some such thing, found him crawling around on all fours muttering."

Cecil turned to Linquist, "Should we be worried about Cecilia?"

Linquist frowned, "Holly is a grown-up. I don't think she'll do anything foolish. Let love live."

"I'm less worried about love living than something dying," Cecil's heart felt heavy, he turned to address everyone, "I didn't want to tell you as I thought it would cause undue concern ... but our guests, well, are more than what they seem."

Fiona held her throat and shivered.

Chas pushed forward, "Bloody hell, what are you talking about?"

"Yes," added Hattie, "What IS going on here? Should I be worried about my Cecilia?"

Freddie came into the room, screwing in his monocle, his hair straight up from sleep, "What have I missed?"

Clemency pulled him over, "Cecil is just about to tell us something about our uninvited guests."

"Thank you darling. Lord Linquist, may I?"

Linquist winced, "If you must."

"To put it bluntly, Lord Linquist, Dr. Tibits, Holly and now, it seems, Professor Janek are vampires."

Hattie roared with laughter, "Come, come Cecil. You must have had one too many. There is no such thing as literal vampires!"

Fiona, realizing what might have happened to her, screamed and pointed at Professor Janek, "Yes! Yes, there is!"

"Young girl I fell on you, I didn't bite you."

Freddie stepped forward, "My god, we must protect the women!"

"Oh Freddie," Jing-Wei said amusedly, "Always the brave one."

Cecil walked over to Lord Linquist, "No, the Lord and I had an agreement, shelter and then free passage if they do not harm us. However, it seems though that agreement has not strictly been kept. Where is Dr. Tibits?"

From the shadows came a low voice, "I am here, I've been here all along."

Lord Linquist turned, "Phillip, come out of the shadows."

"Oh, Sashi," whispered Dr. Tibits, "these people mean nothing to us. Remember the plan? Let us kill them all, what a glorious feast it will be!" Suddenly the room went dark.

"Stop it Phillip, stop it, these people saved our lives, remember? They gave us sanctuary. They are our protectors."

"Sashi, you are a fool! A weak, sentimental fool!"

Fiona bolted for the door but was unable to pry it open.

"No one leaves until we've had this out!" Dr. Tibits shouted, his eyes glowing red in the dark.

Freddie grabbed the fire poker. Cecil grabbed his shoulder, "I wouldn't old man, they are stronger that you. There must be another way out of this one."

"Talk, talk, talk, there's been too much talk!" screamed Dr. Tibits.

Jing-Wei started to scream, "Something is running around me, I can feel them! Like rats...rats!

Everyone leapt and panicked, overcome with the sensation of millions of tiny claws itching and scratching all over their legs. Cecil grabbed Clemency, "It's not real. Feel the pressure of me holding you and focus on that. Focus!"

The windows suddenly flew open and the cold, wet storm raged in.

"Feel my wrath!" Tibits' voice boomed. "I will make a bloodbath of this party!"

"Stop it Phillip! Stop it now!" shouted Linquist.

The fire in the grate exploded, showering a thousand sparks into the room. Freddy grabbed Fiona who began to scream uncontrollably. The howling noise of the storm became unbearable.

"That's it!" yelled Chas. "Something has to be done!"

"No Chas, no!" Cecil cautioned, "This is between Linquist and Tibits, they must battle it out."

"Hanged if I want to wait all night for that, here you bally bloodsucking shadows! Here, feel this wrath!"

"Noooooo!!!!!" the voice hissed followed by a deafening, ripping screech and then a tremendous thud. Cecil ran over to the windows and closed them making the room suddenly, blissfully, silent. The lights flickered back on, revealing the body of Dr. Tibits crumpled on the floor.

"Bloody hell," said Chas, "Did I kill him?"

Lord Linquist knelt beside the body and felt for a pulse. "No, he's just in shock." Looking at Chas he asked, "What did you do? What is that in your hand?"

"What, this? I picked it up off a table. It seemed heavy enough to hit him with but he fell before I could get close."

Everyone turned to look at Chas, who was holding in his hand a large bottle of herbal bitters with silver crucifix printed on it. Cecil walked over and slapped Chas on the back, "Good thinking old man," he said.

Chas looked puzzled.

"I'll explain later," said Cecil.

He then walked over to Lord Linquist, "Can I give you a hand?"

"No, no," said Linquist straining slightly as he picked up the limp Dr. Tibits in his arms, "Remember, we are quite a strong race."

Woolley looked at him "Lord Linquist, after what just happened here, I hope you will not be insulted if I ask you and your party to retire to your craft and spend the rest of the night and day there?"

"Not insulted at all. Can you accept an apology for my friend? He means well…meant well… once. Being eternal, you'd think we'd be the very picture of calm but it seems we all, whether dead or alive, still have baggage to carry."

Chapter Fifteen

Clemency lay back on the bed, "Darling, I want this night to be over."

Woolley, finally getting his nightcap, shook the cocktail shaker furiously and poured out two icy drinks. "Darling, no one more than I wants to be rid of our hellish guests, of this night, of this place and to be back in our hotel between crisp white sheets dreaming of halcyon days."

"I'm just so worried about Cecilia. I think she was quite smitten with Holly," said Clemency. "Oh…look, someone just slid something under the door."

Woolley rushed over and opened the door. The hall was empty. He reached down and picked up a small cream coloured envelope with "Clemency" written in purple ink on the front. "For you darling." He handed it to her and recognizing the writing, she tore it open and read it.

Oh no, Woolley. No!" she sobbed and handed the paper to Cecil.

> Clemency, Our talk today so inspired me. I've decided to finally act with my heart and admit who

and what I am. I am leaving with Holly and her family. I love Holly and want to spend all eternity with her, if she lets me. You know what that means. Please tell mother for me, she won't understand but I know you will. Please don't come looking for me, hoping to change my mind. I am, for the first time in my entire life, truly, truly happy. I will miss you, and Cecil, ever so much. I know one day we can meet again, until then I want to thank you for being the most perfect person ever. The most perfect cousin ever. Please kiss Cecil for me.

Cece.

Cecil tenderly took her in his arms, "Oh Clem, what was that about your family? Soup to nuts?" He pressed his face into her hair and breathing in her scent suddenly felt so calm. Here was where love is he thought, here is where he would build his mansion to be filled with light and shadow and tranquility. Here is where he would plant gardens and a forest green. Here, in Clemency, was his centre, his whole, his reason for being. Holding her, while she silently wept, he reached over to the night stand and taking up his glass, brought it to his mouth and sipped the gorgeous, strong, mysterious, icy liquid — in doing so he felt instantly, irrevocably, at peace with the world.

Chapter Sixteen

Sometime in the pre-dawn hours The Mircalla slipped silently from her safe harbour and out to sea. No one saw her leave, but in the morning when Hattie sent staff down to check on her, she was not there. Gone were the guests and, they assumed, Professor Janek. Gone too was the storm. All that was left behind was a note from Lord Linquist apologizing for being such a concern and to assure Hattie that Cecilia would be fine in their care.

Clemency took Hattie into the library and tried to explain as best she could that Cecilia was following her heart, that she was of age and must do what she must to live her life now. Hattie understood, but not really, and uncharacteristically wept. Clemency put on a brave front but deep down she was sick with worry.

Cecil came and tapped on the door, "Ready old thing? Boat's here." Clemency nodded and kissed Aunt Hattie goodbye, saying she will write, and asking Hattie to send news when she had it and to keep in touch.

The "smart set" and Cecil and Clemency made their way along the dock to meet the boat. They were exhausted and confused; it would take a long time to process what they'd been through this past night. It was as if all the monsters left behind with childhood had come back out from under the bed. However, the day was fresh and lovely, the air filled with the scent of the sea, blown grass and a slight humidity. The ocean was a dark turquoise and there was not a cloud in the sky.

Suddenly Chas pointed at the boathouse, "Good Lord!" Everyone gasped, as in the window within the darkened space, two sets of burning red eyes were staring menacingly at them.

Cecil pushed the girls behind him and looked around for anything that could make a crucifix. Chas, seeing what he was doing, quickly grabbed a grappling pole from the dock and snapped it in two, giving the pieces to Woolley who then held them together to form a cross. "Okay, Chas, when I say the word, throw open the door. Stay back everyone. I'm hoping the daylight alone will be enough to kill them. Are you ready Chas?!"

Chas crouched by the door, "Ready."

"Okay, on my signal, one, two, three … now!"

Chas flung open the door and as Cecil rushed forward, he was instantly enveloped with the acrid scent of marijuana smoke. A voice within shouted, "Hey grand-dad, close the door. What the hay, man!"

Clemency burst out laughing, "It's the missing band! They've been hotboxing in the boat house this whole time!" Everyone on the dock roared with laughter. The musician looked sheepishly out into the light and said, "Oh man, is it time for our set?".

Cecil smiled and closing the door said, "No my good fellow, plenty of time, plenty of time."

Clemency walked over and slung herself onto Woolley.

"Oh, Cecil."

"Yes my love?"

"Life is never dull when we are together."

Woolley chuckled, "No, never dull."

"I wonder what will happen next?"

"The answer to that, my dear Clemency, is that we shall just have to wait and see. For the immediate however, all I crave is a hotel room, a well-stocked bar, you in your knickers and nothing remotely undead."

"My dear Woolley, even I will drink to that!"

The End

David Keyes is the author of over 15 books including *I Do So Worry For All Those Lost At Sea*, An Imagined Autobiography and *The Blood Red Heiress*, which introduced Cecil Herbert Woolley, renowned occult specialist and consulting detective.

Mr. Keyes is also a maker of clocks, curios and coffins as well as a composer, designer and photographer. He lives in Toronto with lots of cats and a skeleton named Basil.

Follow his adventures on Instagram @marlowghost